Hilarious Political Jokes and Satire from the World of Politics

BY

Aaron Remus

It is creative nonfiction, in this case. For various reasons, several parts have undergone variable degrees of fictionalization.

Introduction

The political book is a compilation of witty and humorous anecdotes, jokes, and one-liners about politicians and the political world. This book offers a light-hearted and entertaining take on the complex and often serious world of politics. The purpose of this book is to provide readers with a much-needed break from the seriousness of politics and to bring a smile to their faces. From humorous observations about politicians' public appearances and speeches to witty remarks about their personal lives and scandals, this book covers a range of topics that are sure to make readers laugh out loud. Whether you're a political junkie or simply someone looking for a good laugh, this book is sure to provide hours of entertainment. So sit back, relax, and enjoy the lighter side of politics with the Political Jokes book.

Jokes

1. Why did the politician refuse to eat an apple? He was afraid of being caught in a political scandal.
2. Why did the politician go to the doctor? He was feeling a little Congressional.
3. Why did the politician switch parties? He was trying to find a more lucrative side of the aisle.
4. What do you call a politician who doesn't lie? Retired.
5. Why did the politician visit the eye doctor? He was trying to get a better view of his constituents.
6. Why did the politician wear a mask? He was trying to cover up his true intentions.

7. Why did the politician refuse to debate? He was afraid of losing his temper.

8. Why did the politician go on a diet? He was trying to slim down his approval rating.

9. Why did the politician become a comedian? He realized it was easier to get laughs than votes.

10. Why did the politician refuse to use email? He was afraid of being hacked.

11. Why did the politician join a gym? He was trying to work out a compromise.

12. Why did the politician stop using social media? He was tired of all the likes and dislikes.

13. Why did the politician refuse to visit the library? He was afraid of getting indicted for book fraud.

14. Why did the politician become a farmer? He wanted to sow his wild oats.

15. Why did the politician refuse to take a nap? He was afraid of being caught napping on the job.

16. Why did the politician visit a fortune teller? He was trying to predict the election results.

17. Why did the politician refuse to answer questions from the press? He was too busy dodging them.

18. Why did the politician refuse to ride a bicycle? He was afraid of being labeled a flip-flopper.

19. Why did the politician refuse to take a lie detector test? He was afraid of getting caught telling the truth.

20. Why did the politician refuse to go to the gym? He was too busy lifting weights off his conscience.

21. Why did the politician join a book club? He wanted to learn how to spin better stories.

22. Why did the politician refuse to go on a road trip? He was afraid of going off the campaign trail.

23. Why did the politician refuse to go skydiving? He was afraid of the polls taking a nosedive.

24. Why did the politician become a motivational speaker? He was trying to inspire people to vote for him.

25. Why did the politician refuse to play golf? He was afraid of getting caught in a sand trap.

26. Why did the politician become a chef? He wanted to cook up some new policies.

27. Why did the politician refuse to go to a haunted house? He was afraid of getting spooked by his own record.

28. Why did the politician refuse to take a walk in the park? He was afraid of getting ambushed by the opposition.

29. Why did the politician refuse to visit the dentist? He was afraid of getting a root canal on his campaign.

30. Why did the politician become a stand-up comedian? He was trying to improve his approval ratings.

31. Why did the politician refuse to go camping? He was afraid of getting lost in the woods of his own policies.

32. Why did the politician become a motivational speaker? He was trying to inspire people to vote for him.

33. Why did the politician refuse to go to a water park? He was afraid of drowning in the polls.

34. Why did the politician refuse to go to the beach? He was afraid of getting caught in a wave of public opinion.

35. Why did the politician refuse to go to a bar? He was afraid of getting caught in a scandal

36. Why did the politician refuse to go on a TV talk show? He was afraid of getting caught in a sound bite.

37. Why did the politician refuse to attend a parade? He was afraid of getting caught in a float of scrutiny.

38. Why did the politician refuse to go to a baseball game? He was afraid of striking out with the voters.

39. Why did the politician refuse to take a selfie? He was afraid of the camera adding ten years to his political career.

40. Why did the politician refuse to go to a movie theater? He was afraid of getting caught in a plot twist.

41. Why did the politician refuse to go to the circus? He was afraid of being upstaged by the clowns.

42. Why did the politician refuse to go to a comedy club? He was afraid of being the punchline.

43. Why did the politician refuse to take a taxi? He was afraid of being taken for a ride.

44. Why did the politician refuse to take the train? He was afraid of being derailed by the opposition.

45. Why did the politician refuse to take the bus? He was afraid of being stuck in traffic with his opponents.

46. Why did the politician refuse to go to the doctor? He was afraid of being diagnosed with a political illness.

47. Why did the politician refuse to go to the gym? He was afraid of sweating out his political ambitions.

48. Why did the politician refuse to go to a museum? He was afraid of getting lost in the history books.

49. Why did the politician refuse to go to a concert? He was afraid of being drowned out by the applause.

50. Why did the politician refuse to go to a dance club? He was afraid of being caught in a political spin.

51. Why did the politician refuse to go to a karaoke bar? He was afraid of getting caught singing the wrong tune.

52. Why did the politician refuse to go to a spa? He was afraid of relaxing his political stance.

53. Why did the politician refuse to go to a party? He was afraid of being caught in a photo op.

54. Why did the politician refuse to go to the beach? He was afraid of getting caught in a wave of public opinion.

55. Why did the politician refuse to go to the mountains? He was afraid of being overshadowed by the opposition.

56. Why did the politician refuse to go to the desert? He was afraid of getting lost in the political wilderness.

57. Why did the politician refuse to go to the countryside? He was afraid of getting caught in a cornfield of questions.

58. Why did the politician refuse to go to the park? He was afraid of getting caught in a political dog park.

59. Why did the politician refuse to go to the zoo? He was afraid of being compared to the animals.

60. Why did the politician refuse to go to the airport? He was afraid of being grounded by the voters.

61. Why did the politician refuse to go to the supermarket? He was afraid of getting caught on camera picking the wrong brand.

62. Why did the politician refuse to go to the hospital? He was afraid of getting a negative health report.

63. Why did the politician refuse to go to the gym? He was afraid of being caught on camera with a bad workout routine.

64. Why did the politician refuse to go to the mall? He was afraid of getting lost in the crowd.

65. Why did the politician refuse to go to the beach? He was afraid of being caught on camera with a bad tan.

66. Why did the politician refuse to go to the aquarium? He was afraid of getting caught up in a school of sharks.

67. Why did the politician refuse to go to the church? He was afraid of being caught in a religious scandal.

68. Why did the politician refuse to go to the museum? He was afraid of getting caught up in a history lesson.

69. Why did the politician refuse to go to the theater? He was afraid of getting caught on camera with a bad seat.

70. Why did the politician refuse to go to the restaurant? He was afraid of getting caught on camera with a bad meal.

71. Why did the politician refuse to go to the nightclub? He was afraid of getting caught up in a party scandal.

72. Why did the politician refuse to go to the park? He was afraid of getting caught in a political rally.

73. Why did the politician refuse to go to the comedy club? He was afraid of getting caught up in a joke scandal.

74. Why did the politician refuse to go to the wedding? He was afraid of getting caught on camera with a bad dance move.

75. Why did the politician refuse to go to the funeral? He was afraid of getting caught up in a grieving scandal.

76. Why did the politician refuse to go to the game show? He was afraid of getting caught on camera with a bad answer.

77. Why did the politician refuse to go to the talk show? He was afraid of getting caught up in a debate scandal.

78. Why did the politician refuse to go to the concert? He was afraid of getting caught on camera with a bad singing voice.

79. Why did the politician refuse to go to the art gallery? He was afraid of getting caught up in a cultural scandal.

80. Why did the politician refuse to go to the zoo? He was afraid of getting caught on camera with a bad animal impression.

81. Why did the politician refuse to take a selfie with a supporter? He was afraid of it ending up on social media with a negative caption.

82. Why did the politician refuse to shake hands with a constituent? He was afraid of getting sick.

83. Why did the politician refuse to answer a reporter's question? He was afraid of saying something that could be used against him.

84. Why did the politician refuse to debate his opponent? He was afraid of looking weak.

85. Why did the politician refuse to visit a foreign country? He was afraid of offending the locals.

86. Why did the politician refuse to attend a protest march? He was afraid of being associated with a controversial cause.

87. Why did the politician refuse to give a speech? He was afraid of forgetting his lines.

88. Why did the politician refuse to appear on a late-night talk show? He was afraid of being ridiculed by the host.

89. Why did the politician refuse to attend a press conference? He was afraid of being bombarded with tough questions.

90. Why did the politician refuse to endorse a fellow party member? He was afraid of being associated with their unpopular views.

91. Why did the politician refuse to run for re-election? He was afraid of losing.

92. Why did the politician refuse to vote on a controversial bill? He was afraid of alienating his constituents.

93. Why did the politician refuse to participate in a town hall meeting? He was afraid of being booed by the audience.

94. Why did the politician refuse to meet with a lobbyist? He was afraid of being accused of corruption.

95. Why did the politician refuse to attend a fundraiser? He was afraid of being seen as beholden to big donors.

96. Why did the politician refuse to take a stand on a divisive issue? He was afraid of losing support from either side.

97.   Why did the politician refuse to disclose his tax returns? He was afraid of revealing something incriminating.

98.   Why did the politician refuse to attend a charity event? He was afraid of being accused of using it for political gain.

99.   Why did the politician refuse to apologize for a mistake? He was afraid of being seen as weak.

100.   Why did the politician refuse to retire from politics? He was afraid of losing his sense of purpose.

101.   Why did the politician refuse to visit a prison? He was afraid of being perceived as soft on crime.

102.   Why did the politician refuse to participate in a public debate? He was

afraid of being exposed as unprepared or uninformed.

103.   Why did the politician refuse to work with the opposition party? He was afraid of being perceived as a traitor by his own party.

104.   Why did the politician refuse to take a stance on climate change? He was afraid of alienating his supporters in the energy industry.

105.   Why did the politician refuse to comment on a controversial court decision? He was afraid of angering the judicial branch of government.

106.   Why did the politician refuse to support a proposed law? He was afraid of the negative consequences it could have on his personal finances.

107.   Why did the politician refuse to meet with an activist group? He was afraid of being seen as sympathetic to their cause.

108.   Why did the politician refuse to take a position on immigration policy? He was afraid of losing support from either pro-immigrant or anti-immigrant constituents.

109.   Why did the politician refuse to speak out against police brutality? He was afraid of being accused of not supporting law enforcement.

110.   Why did the politician refuse to attend a public event without security? He was afraid of being attacked or harassed by protesters.

111.   Why did the politician refuse to engage with social media? He was afraid of being trolled or bullied online.

112.   Why did the politician refuse to appear on a reality TV show? He was afraid of damaging his public image.

113.   Why did the politician refuse to take a position on gun control? He was afraid of losing support from either gun control advocates or Second Amendment supporters.

114.   Why did the politician refuse to comment on a scandal involving his party? He was afraid of being seen as disloyal.

115.   Why did the politician refuse to address a racial inequality issue? He was afraid of being accused of playing the race card.

116.   Why did the politician refuse to participate in a photo op? He was afraid of being seen as insincere.

117. Why did the politician refuse to reveal his personal beliefs? He was afraid of being judged or criticized by the public.

118. Why did the politician refuse to make a public appearance during a crisis? He was afraid of being seen as ineffective or unable to handle the situation.

119. Why did the politician refuse to answer a direct question? He was afraid of being trapped by a "gotcha" question or admitting a mistake.

120. Why did the politician refuse to take responsibility for a policy failure? He was afraid of being held accountable or losing support.

121. Why did the politician refuse to attend a public forum? He was afraid of being confronted by angry constituents.

122. Why did the politician refuse to give a press conference? He was afraid of being asked difficult or uncomfortable questions.

123. Why did the politician refuse to criticize a foreign leader? He was afraid of starting an international conflict.

124. Why did the politician refuse to work with a political rival? He was afraid of being seen as weak or compromising his values.

125. Why did the politician refuse to take a strong stance on healthcare policy? He was afraid of alienating his party or constituents.

126. Why did the politician refuse to visit a disaster zone? He was afraid of being seen as using the situation for political gain.

127.   Why did the politician refuse to donate to a charitable cause? He was afraid of being seen as trying to buy public favor.

128.   Why did the politician refuse to take a position on a controversial issue? He was afraid of being seen as flip-flopping or inconsistent.

129.   Why did the politician refuse to meet with lobbyists? He was afraid of being seen as corrupt or influenced by special interests.

130.   Why did the politician refuse to attend a fundraiser? He was afraid of being seen as beholden to big donors.

131.   Why did the politician refuse to take a position on abortion rights? He was afraid of alienating either pro-choice or pro-life supporters.

132. Why did the politician refuse to condemn hate speech? He was afraid of being accused of limiting free speech.

133. Why did the politician refuse to attend a diplomatic meeting? He was afraid of being seen as weak or ineffective in negotiations.

134. Why did the politician refuse to attend a protest rally? He was afraid of being seen as overly partisan or biased.

135. Why did the politician refuse to sign a pledge? He was afraid of being held to a strict or unpopular position.

136. Why did the politician refuse to apologize for a mistake? He was afraid of being seen as weak or admitting fault.

137. Why did the politician refuse to attend a town hall meeting? He was afraid

of being confronted by angry or frustrated constituents.

138.   Why did the politician refuse to comment on a scandal involving his opponent? He was afraid of being seen as engaging in dirty politics.

139.   Why did the politician refuse to take a position on LGBTQ+ rights? He was afraid of alienating either supporters or opponents of equal rights.

140.   Why did the politician refuse to address income inequality? He was afraid of being seen as promoting socialist policies.

141.   Why did the politician refuse to support environmental protection laws? He was afraid of being seen as anti-business or anti-development.

142.   Why did the politician refuse to criticize a law enforcement agency? He was afraid of being seen as anti-police or anti-law and order.

143.   Why did the politician refuse to acknowledge systemic racism? He was afraid of being seen as divisive or promoting identity politics.

144.   Why did the politician refuse to support gun control measures? He was afraid of being seen as anti-Second Amendment or losing support from gun owners.

145.   Why did the politician refuse to advocate for universal healthcare? He was afraid of being seen as promoting socialist policies or increasing taxes.

146.   Why did the politician refuse to condemn a foreign government's human

rights abuses? He was afraid of damaging diplomatic relations or being accused of hypocrisy.

147. Why did the politician refuse to support LGBTQ+ rights? He was afraid of losing support from conservative or religious voters.

148. Why did the politician refuse to support the Black Lives Matter movement? He was afraid of being seen as anti-police or promoting anarchy.

149. Why did the politician refuse to address campaign finance reform? He was afraid of losing support from big donors or being accused of hypocrisy.

150. Why did the politician refuse to support a living wage for workers? He was afraid of being seen as anti-business or promoting socialist policies.

151.   Why did the politician refuse to address systemic issues in the criminal justice system? He was afraid of losing support from law and order voters or being accused of being soft on crime.

152.   Why did the politician refuse to address the opioid epidemic? He was afraid of being seen as promoting drug use or being accused of being soft on drugs.

153.   Why did the politician refuse to address climate change? He was afraid of losing support from fossil fuel industries or being accused of promoting job-killing regulations.

154.   Why did the politician refuse to support immigration reform? He was afraid of being seen as soft on borders or losing support from anti-immigration voters.

155. Why did the politician refuse to acknowledge the impact of colonialism and imperialism? He was afraid of being seen as unpatriotic or promoting a revisionist history.

156. Why did the politician refuse to support the arts and humanities? He was afraid of being seen as promoting elitist or unnecessary expenditures.

157. Why did the politician refuse to support student loan forgiveness? He was afraid of being seen as promoting entitlement or increasing taxes.

158. Why did the politician refuse to address income inequality? He was afraid of losing support from wealthy donors or being accused of promoting class warfare.

159. Why did the politician refuse to acknowledge the need for mental health

services? He was afraid of being seen as promoting a weak or unstable image.

160. Why did the politician refuse to address the need for infrastructure investments? He was afraid of being seen as promoting government spending or increasing the deficit.

161. Why did the politician refuse to address the need for affordable housing? He was afraid of being seen as promoting welfare or being accused of interfering with the free market.

162. Why did the politician refuse to address the need for universal access to broadband internet? He was afraid of being seen as promoting big government or increasing taxes.

163. Why did the politician refuse to support women's reproductive rights? He

was afraid of losing support from conservative or religious voters.

164. Why did the politician refuse to support the legalization of marijuana? He was afraid of being seen as promoting drug use or being accused of promoting a "gateway" to harder drugs.

165. Why did the politician refuse to acknowledge the need for better access to affordable childcare? He was afraid of being seen as promoting "nanny state" policies or being accused of promoting dependency.

166. Why did the politician refuse to support the LGBTQ+ community's right to adopt children? He was afraid of losing support from conservative or religious voters.

167. Why did the politician refuse to acknowledge the impact of income inequality on education outcomes? He was afraid of being accused of promoting class warfare or being seen as promoting a "victim mentality."

168. Why did the politician refuse to support labor unions? He was afraid of being seen as promoting "big labor" or being accused of promoting inefficient and corrupt practices.

169. Why did the politician refuse to address police brutality and racial profiling? He was afraid of losing support from law and order voters or being seen as promoting an "anti-police" agenda.

170. Why did the politician refuse to address the need for comprehensive immigration reform? He was afraid of

being seen as promoting amnesty or losing support from anti-immigration voters.

171.   Why did the politician refuse to acknowledge the impact of systemic discrimination on marginalized communities? He was afraid of being accused of promoting identity politics or being seen as unpatriotic.

172.   Why did the politician refuse to support expanding access to voting? He was afraid of losing support from conservative or Republican voters.

173.   Why did the politician refuse to address the need for better access to mental health services for veterans? He was afraid of being seen as promoting a weak or unpatriotic image.

174. Why did the politician refuse to support universal pre-K education? He was afraid of being seen as promoting "government takeover" of education or increasing taxes.

175. Why did the politician refuse to support a higher minimum wage? He was afraid of being seen as anti-business or being accused of promoting inflation.

176. Why did the politician refuse to acknowledge the impact of mass incarceration on communities of color? He was afraid of being seen as promoting "soft on crime" policies or being accused of promoting a "victim mentality."

177. Why did the politician refuse to address the need for comprehensive gun control measures? He was afraid of losing support from the NRA or being accused of

promoting infringement on Second Amendment rights.

178.   Why did the politician refuse to acknowledge the impact of climate change on marginalized communities? He was afraid of being accused of promoting job-killing regulations or being seen as promoting a "victim mentality."

179.   Why did the politician refuse to address the need for comprehensive public transportation systems? He was afraid of being seen as promoting big government or increasing taxes.

180.   Why did the politician refuse to support universal healthcare? He was afraid of being accused of promoting socialist policies or being seen as promoting dependency on government.

Made in United States
Troutdale, OR
11/01/2023